𝒜
atheneum

ATHENEUM BOOKS FOR YOUNG READERS
An imprint of Simon & Schuster Children's Publishing Division
1230 Avenue of the Americas, New York, New York 10020
Text © 2023 by Linda Ashman
Illustration © 2023 by Karen Obuhanych
Book design by Debra Sfetsios-Conover © 2023 by Simon & Schuster, Inc.
For information about special discounts for bulk purchases, please contact Simon & Schuster Special Sales at 1-866-506-1949 or business@simonandschuster.com.
The Simon & Schuster Speakers Bureau can bring authors to your live event. For more information or to book an event, contact the Simon & Schuster Speakers Bureau at 1-866-248-3049 or visit our website at www.simonspeakers.com.
The text for this book was set in Helvetica Neue LT Std.
The illustrations for this book were rendered in acrylic paint, charcoal, and colored pencils, then finished digitally.
Manufactured in China
1022 SCP
First Edition
2 4 6 8 10 9 7 5 3 1
Names: Ashman, Linda, author. | Obuhanych, Karen, illustrator.
Title: Wonder dogs! / Linda Ashman ; illustrated by Karen Obuhanych.
Description: First edition. | New York : Atheneum Books for Young Readers, 2023. | Audience: Ages 4–8. | Audience: Grades K–1. | Summary: "A look at all that dogs do for us from the extraordinary to the everyday, as told by a dog on a walk with his owner"—Provided by publisher.
Identifiers: LCCN 2022006138 (print) | LCCN 2022006139 (ebook) | ISBN 9781534494534 (hardcover) | ISBN 9781534494541 (ebook)
Subjects: CYAC: Stories in rhyme. | Dogs—Fiction. | LCGFT: Stories in rhyme. | Picture books.
Classification: LCC PZ8.3.A775 Wo 2023 (print) | LCC PZ8.3.A775 (ebook) | DDC [E]—dc23
LC record available at https://lccn.loc.gov/2022006138
LC ebook record available at https://lccn.loc.gov/2022006139

For Jack and Jackson and
our much-loved wonder dogs
—L. A.

To Uggi, Stewie, Lucy, and Mama Kris
—K. O.

Wonder Dogs!

Linda Ashman

Illustrated by Karen Obuhanych

Atheneum Books for Young Readers
New York London Toronto Sydney New Delhi

Look at them!

They leap and chase,

Catch and carry,

Crawl and race—

AGILITY COURSE→

Between the poles,
Into the chutes,
Across the bridges,
Through the hoops.

**Super athletes?
Yes, the best!**

(Unlike me—
I failed the test.)

About their snouts:
They work so well,
They pick up scents
You'd *never* smell.

EXIT →

On land and sea,
They seek and find.
It's tiring work,
But they don't mind—

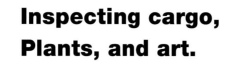

Inspecting cargo,
Plants, and art.

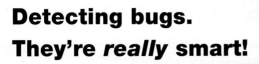

**Detecting bugs.
They're *really* smart!**

They give alerts.
They search and save.
Some of them are *very* brave.

(I'm not so brave—
No daring feats—
But I can sniff out hidden treats!)

They help and herd.
They guard and guide.
They're at your service,
By your side.

GUARD
DOGS
ON DUTY

They're handsome—
Brindled, spotted, sleek,
Wrinkled, shaggy,
Poufed, and chic.

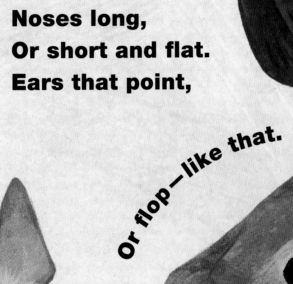

Noses long,
Or short and flat.
Ears that point,

Or flop—like that.

Some grow tall.
Some stay low.

Some are champs—
The Best in Show.

They're Wonder Dogs—
A brilliant crew.

What's that?
What wonders can *I* do?

Me?

Well, yes—
I do not fetch.
I miss a lot when we play catch.

I drool sometimes.

I dig.

I shed.

I have been known to hog the bed.

**Those snacks you made?
I ate a few.**

And, oh—one time I chewed your shoe.

I'm not a champion. Not at all.
I started out alone and small.
At first, nobody wanted me.
But I have talents too!

Let's see . . .

I wake you up.
Greet our guests.
Clean up spills.
Scare off pests.

Make you laugh.
Keep you fit.
(It isn't good to sit and sit!)

I cheer you on a dreary day.
Watch the house when you're away.
Wag with joy when you come back.
(After all, you *are* my pack.)

I listen close,
And keep you warm.

I offer comfort in a storm.

A Wonder Dog?

That's right—me, too.

My superpower?

Loving you.